More Three-Minute THRILLERS

Roller-Ghoster and Other Hasty Horrors

By Eric Elfman

Illustrations by Will Suckow

Lowell House
Juvenile
Los Angeles

CONTEMPORARY BOOKS
Chicago

Other Scary Fare
by Eric Elfman

The Very Scary Almanac
Three-Minute Thrillers

Publisher: Jack Artenstein
General Manager, Juvenile Division: Elizabeth D. Wood
Editorial Director: Brenda Pope-Ostrow
Director of Publishing Services: Rena Copperman
Project Editor: Barbara Schoichet
Managing Editor, Juvenile Division: Chris Hemesath
Art Director: Lisa-Theresa Lenthall
Typesetting: Michele Lanci-Altomare

Manufactured in the United States of America

Library of Congress Catalog Card Number is available

Lowell House books can be purchased at special discounts when ordered in bulk for premiums and special sales. Contact Department VH at the following address:

Lowell House Juvenile
2029 Century Park East
Suite 3290
Los Angeles, CA 90067

ISBN: 1-56565-248-7

10 9 8 7 6 5 4 3 2 1

Table of Contents

*For my mom, who is probably horrified by what I write,
and for Jeff Kenney, who sent me my first fan letter.
Hang in there, Jeff!*
— E.E.

The Stray

Walking home from the store, Becky took a deep breath and smelled the crisp, clean smell of rain-fresh air. She felt the familiar sidewalk under her feet and was glad to be out on her own just like any other independent kid. Suddenly, as she passed an alley, she heard a snuffling sound.

Poor little thing, she thought, as she approached what was surely a homeless puppy, cold and drenched from the rain.

She got about halfway down the alley and then she found it. Bending down, Becky put her hand inside a cardboard box and felt a hairless creature with moist skin. "A newborn puppy!" she exclaimed. "But who would just leave it here to freeze to death?"

She stood and spoke loudly. "Does this puppy belong to anyone?" she asked. "Is there anyone here who knows about this puppy?"

When she heard no answer, Becky turned back to her new friend. "I can't believe someone would leave you out here all by yourself. You're all cold and wet." She quickly took off her sweater and wrapped it around the creature, then picked it up. Instantly the hairless little thing clung to her, shivering in her arms. She shushed it gently.

5

"Well, I'm bringing you home with me," she said finally. And with that she walked determinedly out of the alley.

Becky thought about the responsibility of owning a dog, especially such a young puppy. She hoped that it wasn't too young to be away from its mother, but she saw no other choice. She couldn't just leave it there.

Then she realized there *was* a problem. Her own mother was so overprotective, she had a hard time believing Becky could take care of herself. How was her mother ever going to believe she could take care of another living thing?

As Becky walked along, her doubts grew. *Maybe I can hide it from her*, she thought. *I can hide it in my room, or keep it in the backyard.* "No," she said, sighing heavily. "I should be honest with my mom, and prove to her I can take care of an animal."

As she entered the front door of her house, she shouted, "Guess what I found!" No longer needing her cane, she dropped it in the umbrella stand and made her way into the kitchen. "Can I keep it?"

Her mother, standing at the kitchen sink, took one look at Becky's pet and started screaming. "Drop it! Drop it!" she shouted.

"What's wrong, Mom?" Becky asked urgently. Then she heard her mom open the silverware drawer and search through what sounded like the big knives.

Her mother screamed again, as Becky felt the thing leap out of her arms. She put out a hand to get her bearings and felt the wall next to her. Then, hearing the sounds of a struggle, she started to scream, too.

"Mom!" she cried. "What's happening?"

Blind since birth, Becky was comfortable using her other senses—smell, touch, taste, and hearing—to make her way through life, but she had never heard sounds like these before. She stood frozen in place, listening to her mother's screams of fright, the horrible sounds of gnashing teeth, a terrifying tearing-ripping-rending sound, a crash . . . and finally silence.

"Mom?" Becky called out tentatively, starting to cry. "Mom? Where are you?"

But all she heard was the creature, growling unlike any puppy ever would—and the sound was coming closer.

Don't Go into the Woods

Earlier in the day Neil had told Roger that he heard strange sounds coming from deep in the woods behind his house every night. When Roger asked what was making them, Neil said he was too scared to find out. Of course, Roger wanted to investigate right away, and he used every manipulative trick in the book to get his friend to go with him.

"You have to," Roger had insisted. "Who else can show me where the sounds are coming from?"

So here they were, walking through the dark woods. The only sound they could hear was the wind whistling through the leaves overhead. That alone was enough to give Neil the creeps . . . until he heard what really scared him—a strange, low humming sound, accompanied by a steady, slow drumbeat.

"Is that what you hear at night?" Roger asked.

Neil nodded, his mouth too dry to speak.

"Try not to be so scared," Roger said. "Come on, the sounds are coming from around this bend."

They went around the turn, and a clearing in the woods came into view under the light of the full moon. Roger held his hand up to stop Neil, who nodded, his face grim and his mouth shut tight. Then Roger crept forward and crouched behind a tree. Neil followed right behind.

8

In the clearing, they could see a dozen men wearing masks. Some ancient and frightening ritual was taking place. Two men were beating on drums, and the rest hummed ominously. They all carried long, wicked-looking knives. Roger looked at his friend and grinned. "This is exciting," he whispered. But Neil just stared at the sight.

Then, all of a sudden, the ceremony stopped. The men turned and looked in the direction of the two crouching boys.

"They've seen us!" Roger yelped, wheeling around in terror . . . right into the arms of two men standing behind him.

"Neil!" Roger screamed. "Run for your life!"

But Neil just stood there . . . watching.

Roger stared at his friend, wide-eyed, as the two men dragged him toward the clearing. Neil sauntered behind, relaxed and unafraid. "What are you doing?" Roger yelled. "Run for help!"

But Neil just ignored him and followed the men to the center of the clearing, where they tied Roger to a red-stained tree stump.

Finally one of the men handed Neil a mask and held out a sharp knife. "You have done well," the man said. "You have brought a fine sacrifice indeed."

Neil put on the mask, then took the knife. He moved closer to Roger and whispered into his crying friend's ear, "I didn't want to come back—not with *you*—but you had to insist, didn't you?" Neil smiled, raising the knife. "Now, *you* try not to be so scared, Roger."

Nor Dark of Night

Allison was outside playing when a ghastly-looking mailman suddenly appeared in front of her, holding out a letter.

"Hi," she said, startled. This man clearly wasn't their usual mailman. His cheeks were sunken, his hands were bony, and his eyes stared straight ahead. It was almost, Allison thought as she took the envelope, as if he had died but didn't know it yet.

After the odd mailman left without a word, Allison looked at the envelope's return address and eagerly ripped open the letter. It was from her friend Casey, who had moved away a year earlier, but it was sad news: Casey's parents had been killed in a car wreck. Allison cried as she read the letter, and immediately walked into her house to call her friend.

"Hiya," Casey said cheerily.

Allison couldn't believe how happy Casey sounded. "Oh, Casey," Allison said, "I'm so sorry."

"Sorry about what?" Casey asked.

"About your parents," Allison said, unable to believe how nonchalant Casey was acting. She must be trying to cover up, Allison reasoned.

But then Casey asked, "What about my parents?"

"Didn't they—um, didn't they . . . die?" Allison asked as gently as she could. "You know, in a car wreck?"

"I don't think that's very funny, Allison," Casey snapped.

"*You* don't think it's funny?" Allison asked. "How do you think *I* feel, after you played a prank like that on me? I have your letter right here, in *your* handwriting, telling about the whole thing."

"Liar," Casey snapped. "I wouldn't do such an evil thing. And I won't forget this either. Good-bye!" And with that, Casey hung up and didn't call again . . . until a week later.

This time Allison could hear the pain in her friend's voice, and could tell that her friend had been crying. "My mom and dad," Casey sobbed, "they . . . they . . . *how did you know?*"

Allison nearly dropped the phone. She didn't know what to say and she didn't have to—Casey had hung up.

The next day, Allison had just entered her yard when the cadaverous mailman suddenly appeared once again. He waved another letter at her, not saying a word, and morbid curiosity finally made her take it.

This time, the letter was from her aunt. It said that Allison's uncle and cousin had been in a plane crash and didn't survive.

Allison choked back her tears and re-read the letter. Then her eyes widened: The letter was dated one week away! Somehow she was getting mail from the future!

Panicked, she ran into the house and called her aunt. "Don't let Uncle Alan and Cory go on the plane," she pleaded.

"Now, how did you know they were planning a trip?" her aunt asked.

Allison tried to explain, but knew her aunt thought she was crazy.

A week later, Allison was glued to the TV, watching the news. Sure enough, an airplane crash was reported, and Allison knew without a doubt that her cousin and uncle were on that flight, numbered among the dead.

Allison didn't play outside after that. When the school bus dropped her off, she ran all the way home without stopping. She wasn't about to let that horrible mailman run into her again.

Then, in her room one night, she heard a tapping on the window. It was the hideous mailman, looking even worse than before. She raised the window, and he handed her a thick packet of mail, wearing a grin that sickened her.

In a daze, Allison tore them open one by one. They were all sympathy cards addressed to her parents, from friends and relatives, and they all said the same thing: "We're so sorry to hear about the death of your daughter, Allison. . . ."

Ghost Bridge

"I'm just telling you what it says," said Jake's mom, not looking up from the travel book. "A tornado destroyed the bridge in 1979, and it hasn't been rebuilt yet."

"Well, that's awfully funny," said his father in that patient voice he used just before he was about to lose his temper, "because we're halfway over the bridge now."

They were on a trip to visit Jake's grandparents, who lived over three states away. It was the longest car trip they had ever taken together.

Jake glanced out the back window of the moving car, and his eyes widened. He wasn't sure if he believed his own eyes, so he whispered to his little sister, Drew, "Look out the back window and let me know if you see anything weird."

Drew obediently looked out and gasped. The bridge was disappearing right behind them, as if it were dissolving seconds after they drove over it!

Jake's mother continued to read from the travel book. "Apparently there's a local legend about the bridge," she said. "It says here that once in a while, people do see the bridge. It appears just as it did before it was destroyed, and it lures unwary travelers . . ." Her voice trailed off.

"Where?" asked Jake's dad. "Where does it lure unwary travelers? Where?"

"Just hurry, Dad," Jake said quickly. "Get us over it."

"Come *on*, Dad," Drew begged. "Step on it!"

"Just drive," said their mother tightly, closing the book and shutting her eyes. "Just drive."

Jake's dad looked across the front seat at her, then he glanced back at Jake and Drew's anxious faces. "Well, if this family isn't acting ridiculous," he said. "I have half a mind to pull over right now to talk this out."

The three of them all spoke at once. "No! Keep driving! *Don't slow down!*"

"What does the book say, exactly?" Jake's dad was getting annoyed. "Now that you started it, I want to know."

His mom opened the

book and read the rest of the legend. "It lures unwary travelers to their deaths. But when someone believes in the ghost bridge—really *believes* that it exists—he or she will make it to the other side."

"That's it?" asked Jake's dad, grinning.

"That's it," said his mom, closing the book once more.

"Well, as I figure it," his dad said smugly, "since there are three people in this car who *don't* believe in the bridge, it's all up to me to get us to the other side."

They drove on in tense silence.

"Hmmm . . . that's funny," he said after a few moments. "There *is* something strange about this bridge. It's almost as if I can see the bottom of the canyon through it." He paused and glanced at the family. "You don't think that maybe . . ."

Don't think that! Drew wanted to cry out.

Just keep going! Jake wanted to shout.

Don't start listening to us now! their mom wanted to yell.

But it was too late. All that came out were their screams as the car plummeted to the canyon floor far below.

With the Moon on Their Wings

Cathy and Tasha were exploring a cave near the deserted campsite when they discovered the bats—thousands of them.

Cathy screamed as they flew out of the cave, but Tasha just snorted. "Relax," she said. "They're just ordinary bats."

"I know that," Cathy answered sharply. "They just surprised me, that's all."

"You were scared," Tasha teased.

"Stop it!" Cathy shot back. "I was not."

Cathy had been Tasha's friend for what seemed like a hundred years. Although when they first met she was put off by Tasha's strange ways, once Cathy got to know her, the two were inseparable.

"What kind of name is Tasha, anyway?" Cathy had asked her years before, when they first met.

"It's Russian," Tasha had answered, "short for Natasha."

"Oh, is that where you're from?"

"Near there," Tasha had answered mysteriously, and would say no more about it.

"Look," Tasha said, now pointing to the campsite. "Here comes a car."

"Just in time," Cathy said with relief.

The car parked, and two kids and their parents began setting up two tents.

Cathy was watching the kids, who were looking around the campground. Tasha was paying more attention to the adults, who were having an argument. The mother appeared uncertain about staying in such a creepy place, while the father evidently wanted to stay put.

"Are they gonna stay?" Cathy wondered out loud.

"*Shh*," Tasha hissed.

"Well, excuse me. I'm hungry and I—"

"Quiet," Tasha whispered. "They'll hear you."

It looked like the dad had won, since the family continued to set up camp. Cathy and Tasha smiled.

Later that night, as the kids slept, Cathy bit them each on the neck and drank their blood. Tasha, meanwhile, entered the larger tent and did the same to the parents.

After they had fed, the two felt better. It had been a long, long time since Tasha and Cathy had eaten. So long, in fact, that they were losing their strength to return to human form, the strength all vampires lose when they do not constantly feed.

Cathy fluttered outside the tent, flapping her wings. "I'm so sick of looking like this," she said, flying over to Tasha, who hung upside down from a branch by her talons.

"Be patient," said Tasha. "Once the blood settles into our system, we'll be able to appear human again."

Cathy nodded. "But for now, let's fly. I don't want to be hanging around when the park rangers find those bodies."

And with that, the two bats took to the air and flew away . . . with the moon on their wings.

The Fastest Kid Alive

As soon as Jim walked in the creepy old store, he knew that all the stories he had heard about it were true. All the kids knew and repeated the dark speculations that surrounded the old shop off Main Street, and no kid would dare go in.

It was said that black magic was sold there, and it was only because Jim was so desperate that he decided to go there. Only because he was *really* desperate.

"There's gonna be a track meet at school," he told the odd man behind the counter. "I want to be able to run faster than anyone else. I want to run so fast no one will ever be able to forget it."

"How'd you like to be the fastest kid alive?" the man asked, his eyes sparkling.

"Yeah," Jim said, "I like the sound of that—*the fastest kid alive!*"

The man went to the back of the shop and returned with a pair of wrinkled old sweat pants. He handed them to Jim, who could immediately feel a strange energy pulsing through the soft material.

"Tie the drawstring when you want to start running," the man said, "and untie it when you want to stop."

After haggling a bit over the price, Jim paid the man fifty dollars. He'd intended to pay only half that much, but the pants seemed worth it.

The track meet was the next day. The meet had become the most important thing in the world to Jim, because it was his last chance to prove himself at his middle school. At the end of the year, he would be graduating.

"Not Jim!" the boys would moan when he was the last player left unchosen and the teacher had to assign him to a team. "Unfair!" the chosen team would cry.

But now that he had the magic sweat pants, he was going to make everyone sorry for not wanting him on their team. Now he would leave them all in the dust. *They'll never stop talking about what happens today*, he thought. *Never!*

Jim wore the sweats out to the track loose and baggy, with the string untied like he had been warned. First one set of five boys ran, then another. When it was Jim's turn, he stepped up to the starting line.

"On your marks!" the teacher shouted, and Jim started fumbling with the string.

"Get set!" she commanded, as Jim's trembling fingers finished tying a bow in the string.

"GO!"

Jim was off like a bullet. He was way, *way* in the lead, whizzing by the kids watching from the side of the track. He spotted the line up ahead and crossed it, grinning widely when he saw the teacher click the stopwatch with astonishment.

Then he tried to stop running . . . and tried . . . and tried. . . . But the soft cotton legs of the sweats continued to pump up and down, forcing Jim's legs to do the same.

Jim sped across the field. He could hear the kids laughing and shouting far behind him: "Go, Jim, go!" But Jim was starting to panic. He was already across the field and nearing the school buildings. Two P.E. teachers tried running after him, but there was no way they could catch up. Jim was running so fast it made them look as if they were standing still.

Then Jim remembered the old man's instruction: "Untie the pants when you want to stop."

Afraid he might run into a wall or a tree, Jim reached inside the band of the sweats and pulled the drawstring. But the loose bow he had tied at the beginning of the race became a knot—a very *tight* knot. He tugged at it but only succeeded in making the knot tighter.

With tears forming in the corners of his eyes, Jim tried to pull the sweat pants down, but the evil pants were cinched so tightly it seemed like they would never budge.

He was out of breath now, but Jim still kept running, out the gate and down the street. There was no stopping him now, and there never would be—not the fastest kid alive.

The Troll

Rachel, Pete, and Alex were reading an old book of fairy tales that used to belong to Pete's grandmother when she was young. These weren't the happy, bloodless versions they'd seen in cartoons, but the original, ancient, scary folktales. In this book, Cinderella's stepsisters cut off their toes to make their feet fit into the glass slipper, and the wood chopper cut a bloody slit in the wolf's belly to get Little Red Riding Hood's grandmother out after it had swallowed her alive.

"These aren't the stories I remember reading," Alex complained.

"No," Pete said, touching the book solemnly, "these stories really happened."

"What?" Rachel exclaimed. "Aren't these stories made up?"

Pete shook his head solemnly.

"You're saying fairies and elves and trolls are real?" Rachel and Alex chorused.

"They sure are," Pete answered. "Especially trolls."

Trolls were Pete's favorite monsters in the book. They were huge, hairy, ugly beasts who lived under bridges. And they caught unwary children and ate them alive, then picked their teeth with the children's bones.

"If trolls are real, why aren't there any more around?" Rachel demanded.

"Who says there aren't? Just 'cause you've never seen one—"

"And you have?" Rachel jeered.

Pete paused, then decided to lie. "Sure. I saw one from the car, when we were driving through the tunnel . . . the one down the hill from my house."

"You're lying."

"Am not," Pete said indignantly. "And I can prove it to you—unless you're too scared to come with me."

"I'm not scared," Rachel said nervously.

"Come on, then," Pete said, standing. "How about you, Alex?"

"Uh," Alex stammered, "I've got things to do."

And so Pete led Rachel to the tunnel down the hill, about a fifteen-minute walk from his house. Every once in a while he glanced at Rachel and had to smile when he saw that she was getting more and more anxious with every step they took.

Finally they reached the dark tunnel. A four-lane highway, flanked on either side by a narrow sidewalk, disappeared inside the tunnel's entrance. Cars passing on the bridge overhead made a mighty, continuous roar.

As they stood in front of the tunnel, Pete started to get worried. What was he going to tell Rachel when they didn't see a troll? He had counted on her chickening out. Maybe he could tell her that it was sleeping, or that it had moved on, but then she would know he was bluffing. Slowly, they inched forward . . . and then suddenly a voice called them from behind.

"Pete! Rachel!" the voice echoed off the tunnel walls.

Nearly jumping out of their skins, they turned around to see that it was Alex. "Pete!" he called. "Your mom wants you to come home."

Rachel let out a sigh of relief. Pete was relieved, too. Now he wouldn't have to make up some lame excuse to Rachel. But as they walked back he pretended to be annoyed. "Oh, great," he said. "Just when I was about to show you the troll. Well, let's come back tomorrow. But we'll start earlier, and . . ."

As Pete droned on, around the bend in the tunnel, a troll gnashed its long, pointed teeth and scraped its razor-sharp fingernails against the concrete wall in disappointment. It had been so long since it had eaten.

Well, it thought as it returned to its lair, *at least I'll have a good meal tomorrow.*

Hollowed Ground

It was the second day of camp, and Ted hated everything—especially the nature walks. Now his counselor, Brandon, was leading another one, pointing out one stupid plant after another, while Ted, at the back of the group, bent down to tie his shoe.

Maybe they'll walk off and leave me, he thought. *The way Brandon is raving, you'd think we were walking on hallowed ground.* He lingered over his shoelace as long as he could . . . and that's when the laughter started.

Ted looked up and saw the strangest thing—the path up ahead had turned into a liquid mess, and his cabinmates were standing in it, laughing their heads off.

But all of a sudden, their laughter turned to cries of terror that gave way to panic when the boys realized they were stuck . . . and sinking!

Ted stood frozen, staring at his friends being sucked right into the ground. Their eyes wide with fear, they were reaching out to each other, and worse, reaching out to *him*.

"Please, Ted!" the guys screamed. "Help us!"

But Ted backed away. Some of the guys were in up to their necks already. How could he risk getting near them? What if he slipped in, too? Feeling horrible, Ted turned away as the first boy went under.

Then, one by one, the screams stopped. Slowly,

Ted turned back to see . . . nothing! The path looked totally normal. Horrified, he ran back to camp, screaming and crying all the way.

Ted decided to tell the counselors he'd gotten separated from his group. Ashamed of being a coward, he couldn't tell the truth. Besides, who'd believe him anyway?

But the counselors didn't buy his story. They knew Ted hated camp and was probably lying.

But by that night, when Ted's cabinmates still hadn't shown up, a full-scale search-and-rescue operation was mobilized, and everyone was being sent home.

Anxious to leave, Ted was in his cabin packing when he heard a voice—*Brandon's* voice.

You were supposed to come with us, Brandon said.

Ted stopped, his neck stiffening. He looked around. "Brandon?" he called. "Where are you?"

I'm here, said Brandon, still invisible to Ted.

We're all here, chorused other voices—the voices of the other guys who had disappeared on the hike.

It's fun down here, Ted. Join us!

"No!" Ted screamed. "You're all dead! Go away!"

If you don't come with us, the voices continued, *we'll have to come get you*.

"Look, I'm sorry I didn't help you!" Ted screamed. "I wanted to but I—"

But just then, the ground turned to liquid where Ted stood, and the hands of his friends suddenly shot out of the waiting earth. They grabbed Ted's legs, pulling him down.

Just look at it this way, Brandon's voice rang in Ted's ears as the liquefied earth swallowed him. *You'd never be able to live with the thought of having been such a coward. Now you won't have to!*

Superstrings

"You see, we live in four dimensions," Carl's dad was saying at breakfast. "Three in space, and one in time."

Carl and his mom sat there listening. He didn't know about his mom, but Carl sure had a hard time following what his dad was talking about. He wished his dad would just speak plain English. But Carl's dad was a physicist, so allowances had to be made for him.

"Some of my colleagues think there may be even more dimensions," his dad continued. "One thinks there may be sixteen, and one fellow in England says there could be as many as fifty-six!"

"That's interesting, dear," Carl's mom said. "More coffee?"

"Do people live in the other dimensions?" Carl wanted to know.

His mother smiled. "Carl—" she began gently.

But his dad cut her off. "That's *exactly* what we suspect. Of course, there's been no way to contact them . . . until now." His dad looked out the window. "Now," he continued thoughtfully, "we've discovered things we're calling 'superstrings.' They're incredibly thin—you can't feel them or see them—but they stretch for miles and miles through our universe, and we think they may even go through the other dimensions as well. That's what our experiment at the lab today is about—we're going to try to contact beings in another dimension."

Carl looked at his father in wonder. Was this his *dad* talking? He sounded more like a mad doctor in a science fiction movie. "Can I come watch?" he asked.

His dad looked surprised. "Of course," he said, obviously pleased that his son was taking an interest in his work.

"Will it be dangerous?" Carl's mom asked nervously.

"Of course not," his dad said with a laugh. "We're just making a simple 'phone call,' so to speak, to let them know we're here."

When Carl saw his dad's research center, he was disappointed. It was nothing like the high-tech, chrome-and-white labs in the movies. It looked like just a regular classroom.

A metal box with glass windows stood in the middle of the floor. It almost could have been an ordinary phone booth. A few college students and another scientist were milling around the box, drinking coffee.

Carl's dad introduced him to everybody, then announced, "Shall we begin?"

One student turned off the lights, while another switched on the power to the box.

"More power," Carl's dad said softly. The student at the control board complied. "More," his dad said again.

Then they saw them. Through the window of the box, glowing faintly, then brighter, were thin strands of light.

"*Now!*" Carl's dad nearly shouted. "Double the power!"

The power surged and the box lit up, then the light quickly subsided. Carl's dad nodded, pleased.

"Well, ladies and gentlemen, that ought to let them know we're here! Now we just have to wait for a response."

As the scientists and students conferred, Carl got up and took a closer look at the box. The superstrings inside were still faintly visible.

Suddenly the power surged, and the metal box burst open, sending brightly glowing superstrings erupting into the room.

"Get down!" Carl's dad shouted, but Carl wasn't quick enough. The strings wrapped around him and started to pull him back into the metal box.

"Help," Carl cried as he was being sucked into the box. "Dad, don't let them take me!"

His dad and the others tried, with all their combined strength, to stop the mighty force. But the superstrings, with their super strength, pulled Carl into the box and out of this dimension. Carl's dad banged his fists on the now-empty box and began to sob. His "call" had been answered, sooner than he had expected, by occupants of another universe who clearly didn't want to be disturbed.

It's in the Bag

"Kevin, didn't you hear your aunt?" Kevin's uncle asked sternly. "Take down the trash. *Now!*"

Kevin looked over at his aunt and uncle from where he sat on the couch in front of the TV. He was staying at their house for a few weeks while his parents went through with their divorce, and he was trying to be on his best behavior.

But they just didn't understand. Kevin wasn't being lazy or stubborn. He was scared. Terrified, really. But how could he tell his aunt and uncle what he was so frightened of? How could he explain it when he didn't understand it himself?

One look at their stern expressions and Kevin finally stood up. He went into the kitchen to retrieve the big, wet bag of smelly trash.

"Darn it," he muttered. "The bottom's wet just about all the way through." Annoyed now *and* scared, Kevin made a mental note to be extra careful on his way out to the shed.

The shed. Just thinking about it gave Kevin the creeps. It stood around the back of the apartment building, looking like an ordinary wooden structure, just big enough to hold the six large trash cans for the building. But Kevin knew that the decrepit, cobweb-filled shed was anything but ordinary, and he wanted as little to do with it as possible.

Now, as he approached the horrible thing, Kevin started feeling the same nameless dread that he always felt, and with every step he took, his imagination ran wild.

What if when I open the door a huge, blubbery tentacle reaches out and grabs me? What if a vampire rises from one of the trash cans and bites me on the neck? What if the shed itself is alive, and when I throw in the trash, the door slams shut on me and it won't let me out?

This last thought made Kevin stop. There it was. He was almost there, and he could almost sense it watching him, waiting for him, *waiting* for its chance.

Kevin began pumping himself up for what he would do next. It was the same thing he did the other times he had to bring out the trash. He would fling open the door of the shed, throw the bag toward one of the cans, then spin around and sprint away with a speed that would make a track star jealous. He'd be halfway up the stairs before the door of the shed clicked shut.

But just as he opened the door of the shed, the bottom of the wet garbage bag ripped through. In horror, Kevin looked at the rotting mass that fell to the ground. There, in a hideous, tangled heap, were the carcasses of countless small animals—raccoons, rats, possums—all crawling with maggots.

Gagging, Kevin backed away from the pile . . . right into his aunt.

"We're sorry you had to find out about us like this, dear," she said.

Kevin spun around. His aunt and uncle were both standing there, along with all their neighbors from the apartment building.

"Yes," his uncle said, his eyes shining brightly. "Your aunt and I, well, I admit it, we have . . . *unusual* tastes."

"Unusual?" Kevin blurted, and then, as the people closed in on him, he started to giggle. All this time he'd been afraid of the shed, when all the while the terror was really in the bag.

The Hand Is Quicker

Cody wanted to learn magic more than anything else in the world. But the stupid magic kit his dad bought him was not what he had in mind. *101 Tricks to Astound Your Friends!* the box proudly proclaimed. But his friends not only weren't astounded, they weren't even interested.

Actually, the problem was Cody. He just wasn't a very good magician. He followed the instructions to the letter, but the tricks still fell flat. Once, when he did the disappearing-nickel trick, Terry, the school bully, snuck up behind him.

"Abracadabra," Cody had begun, "the hand is quicker—" But just then Terry had leaned forward without warning and knocked the hidden nickel out of his hand, making a fool out of Cody in front of his friends.

Humiliated, Cody had vowed then and there to prove to his friends that he was a good magician. He was going to show them. He was going to find out how to make things *really* disappear—even if it was the last thing he did!

That's when Cody decided to consult a professional. He went to the scary old antique store off Main Street, the one most kids were afraid to enter, and asked to speak to the owner. *If anyone knows real magic*, Cody thought, *he will*.

"So?" said the owner, coming from the back room. "You want magic tricks, eh?"

"Not magic *tricks*," said Cody, not even wondering how the man knew why he had come. "I want *real* magic."

The owner smiled as he drew a small black case from behind the counter. "Well, let's see what we have here." He opened the bag, and inside Cody could see colorful boxes, ropes, silver hoops, and a thin black rod. The owner pulled out the rod and waved it over an antique vase on the counter. The vase shimmered briefly, then completely disappeared.

"Wow!" Cody exclaimed. "How much for the whole bag?"

"It's cheap," said the man. "Just six hundred and sixty-six dollars."

Cody laughed. "I don't have that kind of money." He paused. "How much for just the wand?"

"Sorry." The owner put the wand down on the counter. "I can't break up the set." He turned away dismissively, and the wand rolled off the counter, landing on the carpet without a sound. "Now go away," he added rudely.

Angry at the rebuff, Cody bent down, pretending to tie his shoe. He picked up the magic wand, slipped it under his shirt, and quickly left the store.

The old guy deserved it, he told himself, *for treating me like a kid.* And soon Cody completely convinced himself that he hadn't stolen the wand at all—he'd just taken it in place of an apology.

As he walked home, Cody could hardly wait to try the wand out. He could actually *feel* energy pulsing through the wand.

He stopped and waved it over a parking meter. "Abracadabra," he said. "The hand is quicker than the eye!"

Instantly the parking meter disappeared. Cody just stood there staring at nothing.

"Boy, am I going to be a hit at school tomorrow!" he said under his breath as he ran home.

The next day at school Cody walked over to his friends. He smiled and pulled the wand out and held it up.

"Now you'll believe me!" Cody announced scornfully. "I'm the best magician in the world!"

But just then, Terry, who had snuck up behind him again, plucked the wand out of Cody's hand.

"No!" Cody screamed as he turned and tried to get the wand back. But Terry just grinned, and waved the wand in a circle over Cody's head.

"Abracadabra," Terry sneered. The last thing Cody heard him say—the last thing he ever heard *anyone* say—was, "The hand is quicker—"

Down the Drain

"It's the pipes," the landlord explained to Ben and Kate's dad when he complained about the noises the family was hearing.

"What does that mean?" Ben whispered to his older sister, Kate.

"Maybe he meant the pipes creak as the building moves," Kate guessed, "or that the wind whistles through them, or—"

"Or there's something *alive* in them," Ben mused.

"Right," Kate snorted. "Like there's a thing living in the pipes!"

"Laugh if you want," Ben said, "but from now on, the only showers I'm taking are in gym class."

Kate did laugh, and she didn't stop taking showers—long, luxurious showers. Sometimes she spent more than an hour in the bathroom. In fact, Kate's showers often caused friction in the household, but there wasn't much anyone could do about it. Once she locked herself in the bathroom, it was all over.

Kate did have to admit that every time she took a shower, she did hear a sound coming from the pipes—a scratchy, slithery sound. But showers were such a luxury for her that she just ignored it. She usually had the radio blaring anyway, so the sound rarely bothered her.

Friday night she was going out to a movie with a guy she liked from school, so she announced to her family that she would take an especially long time in the bathroom getting ready.

"A long time for you?" her dad joked. "How many hours will that be?"

Rolling her eyes, Kate flounced away and locked herself in the bathroom. She turned on the shower and stepped inside the comforting steam, eager to—and then she heard it. It was a scratching and slithering sound that seemed to be coming from right beneath her feet, only this time it was a little bit louder than usual.

Scared for the first time, Kate looked down and gasped. A slimy gray hand with long sharp claws was reaching out of the drain!

"Help!" Kate screamed as she tried to jump out of the shower.

But the thing was too fast. It reached out its skinny arm and grabbed Kate by the ankle, making

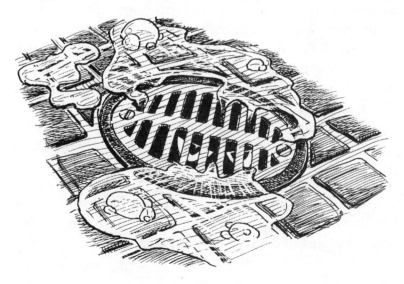

her tumble to the floor. She screamed and screamed, but no one heard her. Her dad was watching TV, her brother had headphones on, and her mom had gone out shopping.

Still in the grip of the slimy clawed hand, Kate rolled on the floor, struggling to get free. Wildly looking around for a weapon, she suddenly had an idea: the can of drain cleaner under the sink!

"Dangerous stuff," her dad had told her. "It'll burn your skin if it gets on you."

Maybe it will burn this thing, too! Kate thought, straining to reach the door under the sink. She flung open the cabinet just as the thing gave a mighty yank, jerking her back toward the shower. Again she reached for the can, and managed to hook her fingertips over the lid, but she knocked the can over and, to her horror, sent it rolling out of reach.

In the meantime, Kate's date showed up and was getting impatient. Ben told him it was typical for his sister to spend hours in the bathroom and suggested that they go outside and shoot some hoops.

Kate's mom came home and started making dinner. Her dad went into his den to get some work done. It never even occurred to any of them that Kate was taking too long. *Way* too long.

Eventually Kate stopped screaming and began to whimper. She struggled a bit longer, then finally passed out. That's when the thing pulled her, inch by inch, into the pipe where it lived.

When her family at last came to look for her, it was too late. They never found her. Too bad no one ever thought of looking down the drain.

Hot Rod

Steve didn't even want to go to the museum, but his friend Brad wanted to see the new exhibit of scary objects—things that had frightening legends or strange folklore behind them. So here he was, looking at the usual museum junk—old bottles, some bones, a piece of parchment—nothing scary at all.

"This is dead," Steve whined. "Let's go."

"Don't just look at the stuff," Brad said. "You have to read about why it's here, too." He pointed at a sharpened bone on display and read the card behind it. "Look at this. It was used for putting curses on people."

"So what," Steve said, yawning. "It's all just made up."

"Maybe, maybe not," Brad admitted. "But it's fun to think about."

"For you, maybe," Steve said. "I'm outta here."

Steve was heading for the exit when one object caught his eye—a thin metal rod about a foot long with a sharp point at one end. Brad glanced at the card, which told the legend of the Evil Spike, an ancient tool used by evil spirits to pierce the black hearts of those possessed to do evil.

Take it, Steve thought, suddenly finding himself wanting to steal it. He shook his head.

"Phew! Where did that thought come from?" But then he noticed that there was no glass case over the spike, and the thought returned. *Take it. You can slip it right under your shirt.*

Steve looked around. No one was in the room with him. Quickly, he grabbed the spike and stuck it under his shirt. *That's weird*, he thought, feeling its comfortable warmth against his bare skin. *I thought it would feel cold.*

Steve glanced around guiltily, then left the museum. Smiling to himself, he started walking home. The metal spike against his flesh was getting warmer, so Steve took it out and put it in his backpack.

"I can't wait to show Brad," he said aloud, chuckling. "He's not going to believe it."

The farther he got from the museum, the hotter Steve felt, even though it was not very warm out at all. *Maybe I have a fever*, he thought. *Great! I won't have to go to school tomorrow!*

Then he realized that the heat was coming from his backpack. He tore it off his back and opened it. Instantly, smoke began pouring out, and Steve watched in awe as his books caught on fire.

"What kind of evil are you?" Steve asked the metal spike, which was now glowing red on the sidewalk—the backpack and books were now no more than ash.

And then a voice boomed behind him as if in answer. "I've waited 400 years to get this back."

Steve whirled around as a tall man strode past him, walked to the red-hot metal spike, and picked it up with his bare hand.

"It was stolen from me four centuries ago by some do-gooder," the man sneered, "and I had to wait until someone with a heart as black as mine stole it again before I could get it back."

The man turned to face Steve. His skin was red in the glow of the red-hot spike. Holding the spike aloft, he took a step toward Steve, smiling, and Steve could see that the person standing before him wasn't human at all.

"And now," the evil spirit said, touching the point of the spike to Steve's chest, directly over his heart, "you shall have your reward!"

Steve wanted to say that he didn't have a black heart at all, that he'd never stolen anything in his life, that he didn't want the evil man's reward, no matter what it was . . . but it was too late. He could see that the man had already given him his reward when he was surrounded by fire and the world as he knew it disappeared.

The Creature Who Eats the Sun

My dad's an anthropologist. He studies the different ways early people lived, and sometimes he travels to distant places, searching for ancient tribes. Once in a while he discovers people cut off from civilization who are still living exactly the way their ancestors lived thousands of years ago.

Every summer when I get out of school, I join my dad at whatever remote site he's studying. This year I met him in South America. He was going back to visit a tribe he discovered many years before. He'd heard that the tribe was dying out, and he wanted to find out what was wrong.

We made the trip together, along with a crew of about a dozen people—a couple of other anthropologists, some of their students, and crew members who carried all the equipment and supplies.

When we got to the village it was nearly deserted, and the few people left were crying. Dad shook his head sadly. "Modern civilization is getting bigger and bigger, Kyle," he told me. "There's less room now for the people who once inhabited this land."

"Why are they crying?" I asked.

My dad talked to one of the other scientists. It seems that the village's shaman was dying. A shaman is like a wizard and a priest rolled into one.

These people had ceremonies for everything—from having a good harvest to having a happy marriage—but without a shaman, the people would have no one to conduct their ceremonies.

"Can't we help him, Dad?" I asked. "Isn't there any medicine we can give the shaman?"

My dad shook his head. He explained to me that the shaman was so sick he would have to be taken out of the jungle to be treated in a hospital in the city, and we just didn't have enough people to spare from the expedition to take him there.

"I know it might sound cold, son," my dad said, "but we're here trying to save an entire community, not just one individual."

That night the shaman died, and the next day there was a total eclipse of the sun. The people in the village, who were really superstitious, started freaking out. My dad said it was because they thought some sky creature was eating the sun, and only the shaman had the special magic to scare it away. My dad must have seen the skeptical expression on my face, because he said, "You shouldn't judge these people by our standards, Kyle. They've had these superstitions and beliefs for thousands of years and don't know any better."

This was the first time my dad ever misread me. I wasn't judging *them*. I was afraid that *we* had been judged by the evil sky-creature for being so stupid as to let the shaman die.

"How long will the eclipse last, Dad?" I asked.

"The longest an eclipse can last is six or seven minutes," he answered.

That was three days ago. The sun hasn't come back yet, and I don't think it will. But we're still waiting, huddling together in the dark, hoping for some light. My dad and the others from the expedition still think the sun's going to reappear any minute now and light up the sky. They refuse to believe what the natives seemed to  have known all along—that the creature is eating the sun because it knows the shaman is no longer alive to stop it.

But I'll tell you, it's not the dark I mind so much. The sun provided more than just light for the Earth. It also provided the heat. And it's starting to get cold. *Real* cold.

Ticker Tape

So what if she couldn't be at the hospital, Carol thought. Her son was in good hands. He had the best doctors money could buy.

It wasn't that she didn't care. She had to work because she *did* care, because she had to pay for his operation. Her son would understand. With the stock market going crazy, up or down a thousand points in an hour, a fortune could be made or lost in the twinkling of an eye. And that's what the operation was going to cost—a fortune.

Carol's son needed a heart donor, and she knew that his doctors would find him one—they *had* to. But for now, there was nothing she could do. The doctors assured her that the life-support system they were keeping him on was all that he needed until they found a heart.

One day, at 9:30 in the morning, Carol got a call from the hospital. Her son had slipped into a coma.

"But, doctor, I can't come over *now*," Carol said into the phone. "I just put in orders for my clients for almost a hundred million dollars. Timing is critical. I have to be here to sell on a moment's notice."

"Of course . . . I understand," the doctor said. "The nurses and I will monitor the situation and keep you posted."

Carol hung up and sat back in her chair. She loved her son more than anything in the world. She would do anything for him. Whether she was there at the hospital or not made no difference; he was in her thoughts.

She hung up the phone and patted the antique ticker tape machine that sat on a pedestal next to her desk. Although it constantly spit out a long, narrow stream of paper with important combinations of letters and figures on them, she hardly ever looked at it. Everything she needed was on her computer. With the touch of a finger she could call up the price of any stock she wanted. Still, it was somehow comforting to hear the quiet burping sounds as the tiny tape was marked by the figures coming through the machine.

Carol stood and moved to her window. From thirty stories up, she could barely make out the hospital where her son lay. She closed her eyes and tried to send him a mental message that she was thinking of him, and that she would be there with him as soon as the stock market closed. *Soon*, she thought, *I'll get a chance to show you how much I love you.*

The ticker tape machine suddenly went silent. "That's odd," she muttered. "It never stops printing—not until the market is closed." She turned to the machine. "Well," she said sadly, "I guess it had to break sometime." She walked over, and while she was looking at the paper, the machine suddenly sprang back to life. But instead of the usual numbers and letters, words were printing out on the thin tape: MOM . . . MOM . . . I NEED YOU.

Carol's eyes widened. She couldn't believe what she was seeing. The tape continued. MOM, it printed out, I'M SCARED . . . IT'S DARK . . . WHERE ARE YOU?

Carol grabbed her purse and ran out the door.

Her assistant looked up in shock as she flew by. "But what about those stocks?"

"Sell!" Carol shouted on her way out of the office.

She ran into the elevator and punched the button for the parking level, where she jumped into her car. But she never made it to the hospital. She didn't see the truck that ran the red light as she pulled out of the parking garage.

When her son woke up a few days later, after his successful operation, the first person he asked for was his mother.

But none of the doctors had the heart to tell him that his mother was there with him always. None of them could find the right words to tell him who his heart donor had been.

Deadly Dirge

Diane didn't want to go into the creepy old antique store off Main Street, but her dad insisted.

"C'mon, it'll be fun. You never know what you'll find."

What they found, and what her dad fell in love with, was an old player piano. They were walking past the huge upright contraption when it started playing all by itself. Diane was startled and jumped back, but her dad was smitten.

"I've always wanted one of these," he said, running his hand along the polished wood, "ever since I was a kid."

Her dad explained to Diane how the mechanism worked. "You take this paper roll here, with the holes punched out, and put it on the spindle, see? Each time one of the holes runs over this row of sensors, one of the keys gets pressed, striking that note, and the song is played."

After some haggling, Diane's dad bought the piano and a bunch of piano rolls. The owner of the shop assured him that his new prize would be delivered the next day.

The piano arrived on schedule, and Diane's father was delighted. Diane, though, continued to feel uneasy around the old piano, although she didn't know why.

"Don't do that," she said to her friend Andy, who came over later that day and started banging on the keys. "It's an antique and worth a lot of money." But Andy ignored her and just kept banging away. Annoyed, Diane walked out of the room. And that's when it happened—the lid came down on Andy's fingers and smashed them. As Andy howled in pain, the piano started playing a tune . . . even though there was no piano roll in it! It was a strange and somber melody, one that Diane had never heard before. In horror, she stared at the keys going up and down all by themselves, as if a ghost were at the keyboard.

"I've heard that music before," Andy said, trembling, as he held his swollen fingers. And then his eyes widened. "It's a funeral march. I'm getting out of here!"

"Andy, wait! Don't leave me here alone with this thing!" Diane screamed, but he was already out the door.

Seconds later, Diane heard a sickening screech of tires. She ran to the door with a horrible feeling welling up inside of her. Andy had run out of the house and across the street without looking . . . right into the path of an oncoming car.

Bursting into tears, Diane ran back to the piano. It had fallen silent.

After that, Diane kept her distance from the piano. But every once in a while, and only when Diane was alone in the house, the piano would burst into the same sad tune she heard the day that Andy had died. Shortly afterward, without fail, her parents would receive news that a friend of the family or a relative had died.

Then one day Diane was doing her homework when the piano started playing the funeral march. Diane had had enough.

"Stop it! Stop it!" she screamed. "I don't want to know when someone is going to die! I don't want to know!"

She ran outside and grabbed the ax from the woodpile, then ran back inside. She rushed toward the piano, with the ax raised above her head. But then she slipped, and the ax flew out of her hand, plunging downward . . . straight toward her heart.

Not a Cloud
in the Sky

Dr. Stilton, the school psychologist, had seen children with phobias—unreasonable fears—before, but never one who had such a strong reaction to something so harmless. Just the sight of one white, fluffy cloud would drive Ian into a state of panic. In fact, Ian's fear was making it difficult for him to be in school. His mother had to bring him early in the morning and pick him up at sundown.

"It started when Ian was playing in the park one day," his mother told Dr. Stilton. "A boy disappeared and was never found. But why would that make Ian afraid of clouds?"

"It was probably a cloudy day," Dr. Stilton speculated. "Your son obviously has connected the other child's disappearance with the clouds."

In an effort to rid Ian of his fear, Dr. Stilton, over a period of weeks, had Ian look at pictures of clouds, then at real clouds through the window. Eventually the boy realized that clouds couldn't hurt him. Soon he was happy to look at clouds and would even laugh at them, almost in a mocking way.

Pleased with Ian's progress, Dr. Stilton decided it was time to take Ian outside. He waited for a perfect cloudy day, but when the time came, he had to drag Ian out kicking and screaming.

"They can't hurt you," the psychologist said, firmly leading Ian out into the yard, ignoring his high-pitched screams and flailing fists. "I promise, there's no reason to be afraid of clouds."

But the little boy was overcome by panic, wailing miserably. "Now," said Dr. Stilton, "I'm going to let go of you, and I want you to stay right here."

He released his grip on the boy, but Ian darted away immediately, running as fast as he could for the safety of the doctor's office.

"Ian, stop!" Dr. Stilton began, then his mouth stayed open in amazement. Four small clouds came down from the sky and surrounded Ian, who was paralyzed with terror. Then, white tendrils reached out and wrapped around the boy's body, enveloping it completely.

At once, the psychologist realized his error— these weren't clouds at all. What the boy had seen that day long ago, the day when the other boy disappeared, were alien creatures of some kind—white, puffy aliens who blended in among the clouds, using them as a sort of camouflage.

In awe, the doctor watched as the creatures lifted the little boy into the sky and carried him off. Then one cloudlike being turned and looked at Dr. Stilton as if to say, *"You're next!"*

The psychologist started to laugh, an insane laugh that would continue for days, and weeks, and months. "You see, Ian," Dr. Stilton kept repeating as he huddled in his office, afraid to go outside, "I was right all along. You didn't have to be afraid of *clouds* after all!"

Slobbering Pine

Tony hated visiting his grandmother. Not because he didn't like her, but because he hated her house. It just wasn't the same since Grandpa wasn't there anymore, and now he hated everything about the old place.

In fact, it kind of gave him the creeps—especially the locked room upstairs that his grandmother said never to enter.

Still, every summer, Tony's parents took him and his sister to spend a month there.

This time, the minute he walked in, Tony remembered the thing he hated most about the place—the loneliness it held for him. His sister kept herself busy reading, reading, reading all day, and his parents played cards or visited with old friends from the neighborhood. But Tony had nothing to do and no one to do it with.

One day Tony was outside walking around the neighborhood when he saw a park with a basketball court. A kid was there shooting hoops. As Tony neared the court, the kid looked at him and tossed him the ball.

"My name's Paul," the kid said.

Tony introduced himself, then dribbled the ball onto the court and started shooting baskets.

The two boys played together for a while, and when the sun started going down, Tony invited Paul back to his grandmother's house.

His parents had gone out to see an old friend, and his sister was nowhere to be seen, so Tony introduced Paul to his grandmother, then took him on a tour of the house.

"What's in there?" Paul asked when Tony went right by the unused upstairs bedroom. "Oh, my grandmother doesn't let anyone go in there," Tony replied. "In fact, she keeps it locked. Try it. You'll see." Paul tried to turn the doorknob, then turned to Tony as he pulled his Swiss Army knife out of his pocket. "It's locked now," he said, grinning. "But I can get it open with this."

Tony hesitated, but Paul eventually convinced him, and soon the two boys stood in the room surrounded by some very odd-looking wallpaper.

Paul's eyes lit up. "Oh, cool!" he said. "Slobbering pine."

"What?" Tony asked.

"I just did a report in school on carnivorous plants—you know, plants that eat insects and things to survive. I've heard they'll even eat a chunk of meat." He walked over and pointed to a plant on the wallpaper. "This is one of them. It's called slobbering pine."

"I don't think so," Tony said doubtfully. "Why would my grandmother have such bizarre wallpaper?"

"But it *is* slobbering pine. See?" Paul pointed at the wallpaper. "The stalks are covered with this sticky liquid. Bugs get stuck in it, and then the plant digests them."

"That's too weird," said Tony. "Let's go ask my grandma why she chose wallpaper with gross plants on it. Come on."

"Nah, you go ahead," said Paul, "I want to look at this stuff a little more. Besides, your grandmother might not like that I picked the lock."

Tony thought about this for a moment, but then his curiosity about the odd wallpaper won out. "She won't be angry," Tony said, leaving Paul there studying the pattern of the wallpaper.

Great, he thought as he went downstairs. *I finally find a friend, and he's a plant freak. Aren't there any normal people around here?*

Tony found his grandmother in the kitchen.

"Grandma, what is that plant in that wallpaper upstairs called? My friend Paul says it's—"

"You went in the room?" His grandmother looked at him puzzled, then her expression turned to fright. "That's not wallpaper, Tony," she whispered. "You didn't leave your friend alone up there, did you?"

Tony looked at his grandmother, then tore up the stairs and into the room. But he was too late.

The tendrils of the plant had already reached out from the walls and had Paul in a tight grip. Paul couldn't scream, because one of the stalks was wrapped around his mouth. The fluids were already doing their work, and he was partly digested.

Tony watched in horror as the plant dragged his friend into its open mouth. "Why, Grandma?" he cried when his grandmother walked up behind him. "Why would you have such horrible wallpaper!"

His grandmother looked sad. "Like I said before, that's not wallpaper. Whatever it is," she said, wiping a tear away, "I—I haven't had the heart to get rid of it."

"But why?" Tony asked in astonishment.

"Because of the last person it ate," she said, weeping freely now. "Don't you see? It ate your grandfather."

Obtuse Angel

As angels go, Stanley was not too bright. If he received instructions that had more than one step, or if something unexpected happened along the way, it was more than likely that Stanley would blow it.

Remember the sinking of the *Titanic*? That was Stanley's fault.

All he had to do was move one little iceberg out of the way, but he got mixed up and moved the wrong one. Another time he was supposed to help guide a scientist toward a cure for cancer but accidentally led him to the cure for dandruff. And once Stanley let the tip of his wing brush against the nose of a worker who was removing fuel rods from the nuclear power plant at Chernobyl. The man sneezed, turning a simple operation into one of the biggest nuclear disasters in history.

Finally the other angels met and agreed that Stanley should not be given any more complex tasks to do. Instead, they decided he should have only one simple job to carry out—a job that had only one step and that occurred often enough for Stanley to get pretty good at it.

The head angel called Stanley in and told him about his new position. It wasn't quite what Stanley had hoped for. In his heart of hearts, all Stanley wanted to be was a guardian angel. Of course, that was the hardest job of all, requiring constant decision-making on the part of the guardian. Stanley knew he didn't have what it took for a job like that. Still, he wasn't quite prepared for this.

He looked down and shrugged his wings. Then, realizing he had no choice, he said to the head angel, "Sure, I'll do it. Why not?" Then he headed off for his first assignment.

* * *

In his bedroom, Timothy was getting ready for bed. He wasn't feeling great and thought that maybe it was something he'd eaten. *Or it could be my nerves*, he thought. *After all, I have a big day at school tomorrow*. The next day Timothy was going to try out for both the lead in the school play *and* for a spot on the baseball team.

Suddenly he heard a sound in his room and turned. A guy was standing there. No, he looked closer, with amazement—not a guy, an angel!

"What are you doing here?" Timothy demanded. "What do you want?"

"I—I'm sorry—" Stanley began.

"Are you my guardian angel?" Timothy asked with wonder.

Stanley was relieved. "Yes. Yes, I am," Stanley said, figuring a little lie wouldn't hurt until he got the hang of his new job.

"That's incredible," Timothy said. "I can't believe it."

"Now, go to bed," Stanley said. "It's late."

"Sure, whatever you say," Timothy said, crawling under the covers. "Wait till I tell everyone at school tomorrow!"

"No," Stanley said solemnly. "You can't tell anyone. This has to be our secret."

"Of course," Timothy agreed. "Does this mean I'll get the part in the play?"

"Yes," Stanley whispered.

"And I'll get picked for the team?"

Stanley nodded.

The young boy was making this very difficult. Stanley would have to stop lying soon and tell the kid the truth.

"Look," he said, "you have to go to sleep—now."

Stanley waited until Timothy fell asleep to do what he had to do. He didn't have the heart to tell the little boy who he really was—the Angel of Death.

Ghoulash

Tom was a loner. During lunch and recess, he sat by himself, never joining in the games of four-square or handball that the other kids played. He preferred to sit by himself, watching. After school he would walk home by himself, and sit and watch TV.

When the new girl came into class, Tom could tell she was a loner, too. She made no effort to make new friends and actually rebuffed the efforts of the other girls to become friends with her.

As often happens with fellow loners, Tom and the new girl gradually became aware of each other. Each time they went to watch the others play, they found themselves sitting closer and closer together. Eventually they began talking to one another, and very soon the two realized that they weren't exactly loners anymore—they had each other.

Tom's new friend's name was Cassy, and she and her family had just moved from a town in the Midwest. "My family moves a lot," Cassy said. "I've learned not to make friends, because I know I'm never going to see them again."

That made Tom sad, but he decided to enjoy Cassy for as long as he could. And so the two became inseparable. In fact, the idea of going back to his life as a loner made Tom really upset.

One day, he invited Cassy over to his house after school. She met his parents, and they liked her as much as he did. His mom even asked her to stay for dinner.

But Cassy quickly refused. "I'm on a restricted diet," she explained. "I have to go home to eat."

After that Tom realized he never saw Cassy eat anything—not at school during lunch, not at the mall after school—never.

"What is it? Are you sick?" he asked.

"No, nothing like that," she said. "There are only certain foods I can digest. My whole family is the same way."

So Tom was nervous when Cassy invited him to dinner. "So what are we going to have?" he asked. "I mean, am I going to like these 'certain foods'?"

Cassy seemed a little sensitive about it. "Don't worry," she said. "Just come home with me after school. We can hang out till dinner."

But as they were walking back to her house after school, Tom started worrying. What *were* they going to eat? Something like sweetbreads—what were those again? The brains of a lamb or something? *Gross!*

"Tom," Cassy began as they were walking along, "I really like you, and when we have dinner I'm going to tell my parents—"

"Look," Tom said, putting his hands up, "if you're going to be introducing me to your parents as your boyfriend, I have to tell you right now that I consider us just friends."

"Okay," she answered, looking down. "But that's not—"

"Listen, I can see I've upset you. Maybe I should just hold off on meeting your folks," Tom said, glad for the excuse to get out of dinner. "I'll see you tomorrow."

Tom left before Cassy had a chance to say another word. He glanced back only once and saw her looking at him. She looked sad, but also, he thought, oddly relieved.

"Well, where's your friend?" Cassy's mother demanded as she walked in. "I thought we were having him for dinner."

"He's not coming," Cassy answered.

"Oh, great," her father said, coming out of the kitchen, picking his sharp teeth. "Now we have nothing to eat."

Cassy's mother turned to her husband. "What about that nice young man from your office?" she asked.

"Nah," her husband said, sneering. "We finished him last night."

Squeaky Clean

"Did you wash your hands?" Jamie's father asked. "I want them squeaky clean."

Jamie nodded.

"With Cleanso soap?"

Jamie paused, then nodded again.

Her father raised his eyebrows. "Let me see them."

There was nothing Jamie could do. She held out her hands.

Her father took one look at them, gave them a whiff, and yelled, "Get back into the bathroom and wash your hands with that soap!"

"I don't wanna," Jamie whined. "I don't like the way it makes my hands feel. Can't I just use your soap?"

"Now look, Jamie, you were so upset when we ran out of Cleanso last time that we bought a whole case of it." Her father looked at her sternly. "I've just about had it with you and this nonsense about that soap."

After she left the living room, Jamie's dad turned to her mom. "What do you suppose is with that kid?"

"Oh, don't worry about it," her mom said absently. She was listening to a radio talk-show as she bent over some work she had brought home from the office. "Kids change their minds all the time. Next week she'll be dying to use Cleanso again."

"Well, that soap is expensive," Jamie's dad said. He stood up. "I'm going to see that the bath she takes tonight is with Cleanso. She has to learn that money doesn't grow on trees."

And with that he walked straight to the bathroom and filled the tub with water, holding the bar of Cleanso under the running faucet so the bath would fill with suds. He nodded with satisfaction as he felt his hand get tingly. *That's what cleanliness feels like,* he thought. He looked at the bar of soap shaped like a monster and shook his head. *No wonder kids today are crying for this stuff.*

Jamie's dad rinsed his hand off and stepped into the hall.

"Jamie!" he shouted.

Jamie stepped out of her bedroom and looked at him. "What?" she asked.

"I've got a bath ready for you, full of that Cleanso soap that you just had to have last week. Now I want you to jump in."

Jamie looked scared. "But—"

Jamie's dad cut her off. "No buts! That soap is expensive, and it's not going to go to waste just because of your silly whims."

Jamie reluctantly went into the bathroom, shut the door, and locked it. Her father, listening through the door, heard her get into the tub. Then he heard her sobbing.

"Dad, I don't like it! It doesn't feel good! It tingles!"

"That's enough whining," her father said, shaking his head. "It's only soap, Jamie. It's only soap."

Still, feeling a little guilty, he stood outside the bathroom door to make sure she stopped crying. It took about fifteen minutes, but finally she stopped.

"Frank! Frank!" His wife shouted at him hoarsely from the living room.

"What is it?" he asked. "Why are you shouting like the house is on fire?"

She came rushing down the hall toward him. "I just heard on the radio that there was some kind of accident at the factory where they make Cleanso soap. It was contaminated with radioactive waste! If you get it on your skin, it's deadly!" Her eyes grew wide. "Where's Jamie?"

Her husband stared at her. His mouth was opening and closing, but no words were coming out.
He pointed at the closed bathroom door,
through which not a
sound—
not even a
squeak—
could be
heard.

Thirsty Engine

The big old car pulled to a stop in front of the school, and Tina reluctantly stepped away from her friends.

"Gotta go," she said. "My carpool's here."

"Carpool?" asked Rachel. "You're not taking the bus anymore?"

"No, my mom didn't want me walking home from the bus stop alone," Tina said, hurrying toward the car. "See you tomorrow!"

The other kids in the carpool had already piled into the back. *Why do they look so tired?* Tina wondered. *They must have had a rough day at school.*

She climbed into the passenger seat and looked over at elderly Mr. Webster, the driver. He didn't have a child, but he had volunteered to help out their parents by driving a few days anyway.

"Oh, it's no bother," Tina had heard him telling her mom. "What else do I have to do with my time?"

Mr. Webster put the car into gear, then glanced at the fuel gauge. "I hope you don't mind if we stop at the filling station. This car sure is thirsty." He pushed a cassette into the tape deck, and Tina closed her eyes. The next thing she knew, she was home.

"How was the first day of carpool?" Tina's mom asked as she walked into the kitchen.

"Fine," Tina shrugged, still groggy. "I guess."

The next day Tina's mom drove the kids to school. Another kid's dad drove after that. Then it was Mr. Webster's turn again.

"Gotta go back to the filling station," Mr. Webster said as they pulled away from the school. "I've never seen such a thirsty engine."

As Mr. Webster reached forward to slide a cassette into the tape deck, Tina, sitting in the backseat right behind him, slipped the headphones of her portable cassette player over her ears.

That's when she saw the other kids in the car pass out. She took one of the earphones off her ear and heard the weird, hypnotic music that was coming from the car's speakers. *Could that be what's knocking them out?* she wondered.

Suddenly Tina could feel the music beginning to put her into a trance. She quickly put the earphone back on, and when Mr. Webster glanced into the back, she pretended to be asleep.

Mr. Webster drove the car to a garage at the edge of town and pulled inside. Tina watched through half-closed eyelids as he got out of the car and opened the hood. *What is he doing?* she wondered.

Then she saw them—four slithering arms snaking their way from the hood through the car's open windows. Three of them attached themselves to the other kids' necks. When the fourth came for Tina, she couldn't help herself—she screamed.

"She's awake!" Mr. Webster shouted, racing to Tina.

"Grab her!" commanded a voice from under the hood.

Mr. Webster raced to Tina's side of the car, pulled her out, then dragged her toward the front of the car. That's when Tina got a glimpse under the hood. There, where the engine should have been, was a vile creature, pulsating and covered with gray slime. A mouth opened in the center of the monstrous engine, and small bubbles formed in the slime as it spoke. "Hold her arms," the quivering thing said to Mr. Webster, as it released the sleeping kids in the car and attached itself to Tina's neck.

"Please," Tina begged Mr. Webster, "make it let me go."

The thing in the car laughed—a deep, bubbling, nauseating sound. "Don't bother talking to him; his mind is gone. I control him now."

Tina felt four stings on her neck.

"I've been staying alive," the thing continued, "by taking little sips of blood from your friends." It made a contented sound. "But now, finally, *you* will quench my thirst."

Framed

"But it's an antique, dear," Hillary's mother insisted, admiring the small gold frame. "It's over two hundred years old."

"Come on, Mom, please," Hillary said, pouting. "It's an ugly old frame, and I don't want you putting my picture in it."

Hillary's mother fumbled in her purse for her notes. She had written down what the antique dealer had told her about the frame—or at least she tried to. The man had spoken so fast she had trouble keeping up. "The antique dealer on Main Street had said it was made for the palace of Louis XVI, in France," her mother explained. "Years later, it turned up in Russia, where Rasputin used it to display a portrait of the czarina."

"Boring," Hillary said, yawning with exaggeration.

"Hardly," her mother continued. "Rasputin was a mad monk. Then it belonged to Aleister Crowley, who was a famous witch."

"Warlock, Mom," Hillary corrected. "Male witches are called warlocks."

Hillary was still putting up a resistant front, but she had to admit to herself the frame was sounding more interesting.

"Well, whatever," Hillary's mother said, looking up from her notes. "I'm just telling you what the antique dealer told me." She glanced back down at the paper in her hand. "Hmm . . . somewhere along the way the frame acquired a . . . I can't read my own handwriting."

Hillary took the pages from her mom's hands and struggled to read the scribbled notes. "I think it says that the frame is—what is this word? *Charmed?* Anyone who puts their picture in the frame . . . Oh, I can't read it, but it says something about being the same age forever."

"Yes," her mother said, taking the paper back. "I think it says something like that."

"All right, then," Hillary finally relented. "Put my picture in the frame. We'll see if it works." She smiled. "I wouldn't mind staying thirteen forever."

The next day at school, Hillary had trouble keeping up in P.E. She got very tired walking home from school, and when she got home she went right to her room and collapsed into bed.

73

Worried, her mother was looking for the doctor's phone number when the phone rang. It was the antique dealer.

"So how do you like the frame?" he asked.

"Oh, very much, thank you, but I'm sorry, I have to call the—"

"Did you decide to ignore the curse after all and put your daughter's picture in the frame?"

"Curse? Oh, that was the word. We thought it was 'charmed.' But why would staying the same age be a curse?"

"Oh, you misunderstood," the dealer said. "The curse is whoever's picture is in the frame becomes the same age—*as the frame*."

Hillary's mother froze, then dropped the phone. She ran upstairs and screamed. There, in Hillary's bed, lay a stranger.

"Where's my daughter!" she screamed. "Where's Hillary?"

But the old woman lying on the bed was too senile to speak.

Hillary's mother stared at the old crone with alarm. She didn't think she had ever seen anyone who looked that old. Why, the woman looked like she must have been over two hundred years old!

Tiny World

I used to loved my little village. All day, for hours and hours, I would happily chase my friends, and they would chase me. Round and round we would go, running in a circle, never getting tired. Life was simple then. We had no cares or worries. Our little village was small, but it was home.

A river flows nearby our village, and strangers come by in a never-ending stream of small boats. I guess they think we are "cute," living our simple lives, wearing our native costumes, and singing all day long. Some of them even try to sing along with us.

Life has always been predictable and routine, but we never used to be bored. We knew what each day would hold: the song, the circle, and the tourists floating by. Truly, we were happy . . . until the day our whole world changed—the day a boy in one of the boats stood up and fell in the water.

We couldn't believe it. He *stood up*. Something different had happened; something had changed.

We kept singing and laughing and running in circles, like we always do, as the line of boats suddenly came to a standstill and men came to help the boy out of the water. Still, the boats did not move. It seemed the boy's hat had fallen in the water and

gone under one of the boats. None of the boats could move until they found the hat. A command was given, and *all* the people in the boats stood and were taken off one by one.

We were shocked. We had always felt superior to the people in the boats because we thought they had no legs. But now we could see they not only had legs, they didn't have to stay in the boats. They could walk wherever they wanted to go.

We couldn't do that. We couldn't stop singing and running in circles. Suddenly, for the first time, I became aware of the way my feet were bolted to a metal plate in the floor that was turning me around and around. Now I was aware of the machinery that moved my arms up and down, forcing me to move without regard for what I wanted to do. The smile painted on my face allowed me to express no other feeling either. With this knowledge, I was no longer happy. In fact, I was mad.

After a little while, the boats started moving again. Streams of endless visitors once again continued to float past us, staring at us. But everything's different now.

Now I hate the visitors. We *all* do. Oh, we continue to sing and smile, but in our hearts the hatred burns. As we run around in our never-ending circle, with smiles painted on our faces, we plot and plan for what we will do the day we can move. I try every day, and every once in a while, little by little, I can feel the screws that hold my feet to the metal plate in the floor coming loose. And the others are doing the same. The day is coming when we will break free.

Perhaps that will be the day that you are riding in the boat, the day you come to visit me.

See Monster

Sally loved the cool darkness under the boardwalk. When it got too hot on the beach and she didn't feel like going in the water, that was where she loved to go. While everyone on the beach was walking like a chicken on the hot sand, or risking sunstroke above on the burning boards, she was cool and safe and hidden underneath.

Rick was down there with her today. He never went under the boardwalk without making a fuss, though, and Sally thought he was a real scaredy-cat. He'd always moan and complain about how dark it was, and how there might be spiderwebs and all that. But eventually he'd always give in.

After their eyes adjusted to the dark, they would start exploring, poking into the dark corners under the boardwalk, hoping to find a pirate's treasure or a piece of a shipwreck. All they ever found, though, were the occasional dimes and nickels that had fallen through the spaces between the boards above, along with a lot of cigarette butts, napkins, wooden ice-cream spoons, and other litter that people dropped as they enjoyed the sunny days.

But today was different. Today, when Sally and Rick were digging in the sand under the boardwalk as usual, Rick suddenly gasped at something.

"What?" Sally asked impatiently.

"I touched something weird, something sticky," Rick said, drawing back.

"Let me see," Sally said, sticking her hand in the hole Rick had dug. She touched it, too, but not afraid like he was, she began digging around the thing, widening the hole and making it deeper.

"Can you see what it is?" she asked, squinting. Light came in thin bands under the boardwalk, but none fell directly on the hole.

"No," Rick said.

"It's long and thin and slippery, and there's something that feels like suction cups on one side," Sally began. "But I can't—"

"It's a tentacle!" shouted Rick, excited. "We found an octopus!"

The two of them started digging faster.

"This is cool," Rick said. "We can bring it to school. We'll get extra credit."

They kept digging and digging until it was getting late. In fact, the two of them were sitting in the hole now, and the tentacle looked to be about four feet long, with no sign of an end to it.

"How long do you think it's been here?" Rick asked.

"I don't know," Sally answered. She felt that something was wrong, but couldn't figure out what.

"It can't have been here very long," Rick said. "It hasn't rotted at all. It must have just died."

That's it! Sally thought. *That's what's wrong! Just because it hasn't moved and is covered with sand doesn't mean it isn't alive!*

"Look out!" Sally shouted, jumping from the hole. "It may be—"

But Rick didn't move fast enough. The tentacle wrapped around his neck and squeezed, not even giving him the chance to scream before it began disappearing into the sand, pulling Rick after it.

But Sally was sure screaming now, holding onto Rick's waist, then his legs. Finally only his feet were sticking out of the hole. Sally tried to hold onto them, but soon he was gone, and Sally was left holding nothing but one of Rick's old sneakers.

She kneeled there sobbing . . . and never even saw the second tentacle under the boardwalk, reaching out from the darkness for her.

Don't Be Rash

Mrs. Stormer, the fifth-grade teacher, missed the meteor shower because she was out of town for a family emergency. When she came back the next day, her class told her about the unexpected spectacle, and how the whole town had turned out to see it.

Seeing her students' excitement, Mrs. Stormer decided to delay the lesson she had planned on the Pilgrims and explore her students' newfound interest in astronomy. One day, while in the middle of explaining the difference between a meteor and a comet, she had to stop. Alfred's scratching was disrupting the whole class. She immediately asked that everyone read a page in their science book, and then she walked over to his desk.

"Alfred, are you all right?" Mrs. Stormer quietly asked him.

"Yeah, sure," he said, scratching his chin vigorously.

Mrs. Stormer frowned. "But what's all this scratching about?"

"Oh," Alfred said, shrugging, "I've got some kind of rash. It's no big deal."

But when she saw the gray-green blotches that mottled his chin, as if a fungus were growing there, Mrs. Stormer backed away. "Uh, you need to go to the nurse. Maybe she can put something on that rash."

The next day Alfred was no better. In fact, two other kids had the mysterious rash now. Melissa, who sat across from Alfred, scratched her long arms, and Bob, who sat behind her, scratched and scratched his shoulders and chest. Mrs. Stormer was driven to distraction and was unable to focus on the lesson she was trying to teach. Finally she gave up and handed out worksheets for the kids to complete.

By the middle of the week, nearly half the class was scratching, and Mrs. Stormer was at her wit's end.

"Maybe it's something in your classroom," the principal suggested when Mrs. Stormer mentioned it to him at lunch.

"Or it could be a mild form of mass hysteria," proposed the nurse, scratching the back of her head.

"Well, keep me informed about it, will you," concluded the principal, scratching his neck.

That afternoon, Mrs. Stormer looked around the teacher's lunchroom. *All* the other teachers were scratching.

And, by Friday, every kid in the class was scratching. Mrs. Stormer could hardly contain herself. She was beginning her lesson on the Pilgrims and was holding the model of the *Mayflower* she always used when Alfred, scratching like crazy, actually peeled off all the skin on his chin.

The boat model slipped from Mrs. Stormer's fingers, and she opened her mouth to scream.

"What's wrong, Mrs. Stormer?" Alfred asked, his jawbone now visible, moving up and down above the flap of skin.

Mrs. Stormer looked around the room in horror. The skin on Melissa's arms was peeling off. The other kids, too, were losing their flesh. Mrs. Stormer could see glistening bone and exposed muscle everywhere.

She put her hand over her mouth and stumbled out of the classroom into the hall.

"What's wrong, Margaret?" the principal asked, coming toward her. The skin on his neck was completely gone.

Mrs. Stormer stared at him. She could plainly see his esophagus and his Adam's apple freely bobbing up and down. "What's wrong?" she repeated. "Am I the only one not coming out of my skin?"

"Now, don't be rash," cautioned the principal. "You're falling apart."

"*I'm* falling apart?" Mrs. Stormer nearly exploded. "*I* shouldn't be rash?" She was still laughing hysterically as the ambulance took her away.

Dead Man's Handle

"Breaker, breaker, this is Boy Wonder. Anyone out there?"

Glen was sitting in the driver's seat of the old black car parked in the steeply sloped driveway behind his house. It was his dad's car, the one he drove when he wasn't working . . . before the accident.

Glen's dad had been a trucker. He used to drive a big rig around the country until that horrible night, months ago, when his mom had gotten the call telling her he'd been in an accident. Glen distinctly remembered the way his mom had slumped against the wall, and he had known instantly that his dad wouldn't be coming back home ever again.

Now he and his mom lived alone, way out in the country, far from any other house, making it hard for Glen to see his friends very often. Before the accident, that didn't matter. When Glen got lonely, he'd sit in his dad's car, get on the CB radio, and try to contact him on the road. Now when Glen was lonely, he sat in the car looking for *anyone* to talk to. He used the handle, or nickname, his dad had given him years ago—Boy Wonder.

"Breaker, breaker. Boy Wonder here," Glen said into the mouthpiece. "Anyone out there? Over."

Suddenly a voice crackled back at him through the speaker. "I read you, Boy Wonder. Loud and clear. Over." The voice was familiar.

"Who am I talking to?" Glen asked.

"Who are you talking to?" The astonishment in the voice was obvious. "This is Red Dog, you lunkhead."

Glen sat up straight in the seat. *Red Dog?* The hair rose on the back of his neck. That was his *dad's* handle.

"Are you there, Boy Wonder?"

"Is—is that you, Dad?"

"Sure is. I'm coming to—" The voice broke up in a crackle of static.

"But Dad, you're—" Glen couldn't bring himself to say the word.

"Late? I know, son. Couldn't be helped. But I'm on my way now. I'm on Pine Ridge Road."

Pine Ridge? Glen thought quickly. *That's less than a mile away.*

Glen's mom wouldn't talk to him about his dad's death, but Glen found out it had been a horrible accident when he read a letter his mom had written to her sister. Apparently his dad was so mangled, his mom could identify the body only from the shirt he was wearing.

"I'll be there soon, son. You still reading me?"

Glen looked down the road and saw headlights coming. "But Dad, I—I don't—"

"No buts, boy. Sit tight and don't move. Everything's going to be okay."

The headlights were getting closer. They were

definitely the headlights from a big rig. Glen watched, his heart pounding.

Suddenly the brakes of the old car gave out. In a split second, the car rolled down the steep driveway and out onto the country road, where it came to a stop. Glen scrambled for the driver's side door and pushed, but it didn't budge—no one had driven the car for so long the door was jammed.

Now the enormous headlights were almost upon Glen. But then, from the *opposite* direction, he heard the shrill blast of an air horn. He turned just in time to see *another* set of headlights closing in on him! *I'm about to be crushed between two trucks!* Glen's mind screamed.

He turned back and saw the first set of head-lights swerve out of the way to avoid the other oncoming truck. Then the huge red big rig whooshed by, missing the car Glen was in by inches.

Glen spun around and saw the *second* set of headlights almost upon him. He raised his eyes to the cab and saw a familiar face—it was his dad! Then, just before it reached him, the truck suddenly vanished.

"That was a close call, good buddy," his dad's voice crackled over the CB. "Next time you're on your own. Don't forget to push that old car off the road. Over and out."

"Dad!" Glen cried into the radio. "Dad!"

But the radio in his hand was dead, and Glen was overcome with grief, for he knew that his dad had come back for one last job, and now it was over.

Grounded

Kyle's parents warned him that when his grandfather came to stay with them, Kyle's behavior was going to have to change. He would have to obey his elders and show respect, because his grandfather wouldn't stand for the kind of nonsense Kyle's mom and dad put up with.

"Your grandfather is quite strict, Kyle," said his mom. "Very traditional. He does things the old way. That's just the way he is, and he's not going to change."

Kyle snorted, not even bothering to turn away from the TV, but he noticed his mother wasn't just doing her normal pleading routine—she actually sounded scared. *Well,* he thought, *we'll see just how strict the old man is.*

And so, from the minute they picked his grandfather up from the airport, Kyle began testing him, doing all he could to push the limits of the old man's patience. He played his music as loud as he could and invited his friends over, even though he was told his grandfather needed peace and quiet. And, worst of all, he answered back rudely whenever the old man asked him anything.

His grandfather stared at him with a nerve-shattering glare. "I'm warning you," he said, shaking a bony finger at Kyle. "Behave, or you will have to be grounded."

Kyle laughed right in his grandfather's face. "*Ground* me? Is that the best you can do?" Kyle snorted. "I thought you were supposed to be tough."

"Grounding doesn't scare you, huh?" his grandfather asked, surprised. "*I* sure wouldn't want to be grounded."

"*I sure wouldn't want to be grounded,*" Kyle mocked.

"Look, I'm warning you," his grandfather repeated sternly. "One more chance is all you get, then I *will* ground you."

"Papa means it, Kyle," his mother said, tears welling up in her eyes. "Really. Please don't disobey him. Tomorrow is our big family picnic—all my brothers and sisters are coming with their families to see Papa—and I want you to be there."

But Kyle, wearing his headphones, just turned his music up louder.

I hope I do get grounded, he thought. *Who wants to go to a silly old picnic anyway?*

So, the next time he had a chance, Kyle snapped at his grandfather, showing him no respect at all.

His grandfather shook his head. "So you're ignoring my warning after all. Now I have no choice. I'll have to ground you."

"Yeah," Kyle said, smirking. "Like I'm really scared. *Ooh* . . . I'm shaking."

* * *

The next day was the family picnic, and dozens of people were milling around the big yard. Kids were eating hamburgers fresh off the grill, and food and drink were plentiful. But Kyle wasn't there.

Kyle's mom sat off by herself, rocking back and forth. She turned away when one of the children carried out a platter of raw patties for the grill.

In the kitchen, Kyle's grandfather, who did things the old-fashioned way, was grinding the meat for the hamburgers himself.

I don't understand it, he thought. *I don't know why the boy wouldn't listen.* He shrugged and fed more meat into the opening of the old grinder. *I kept warning him I'd ground him,* he thought as he slowly turned the crank. And that's exactly what the old man was doing . . . right that very minute.

Roller-Ghoster

Ken loved roller coasters, especially really scary ones. In fact, he tried to make the rides even scarier by unbuckling the seat belt or wedging his leg under the protective metal bar to keep it away from him.

Of course, it was behavior like this that had led to the accident . . . but Ken always managed to push thoughts about that away. It wasn't his fault, he told himself over and over again until he believed it. It just couldn't have been his fault.

And so, his love of roller coasters never ended. That's why he was thrilled when he received an invitation to visit a new amusement park being built near his house, *before* it opened to the public.

THIS INVITATION IS FOR *YOU* ONLY, the card read. COME ALONE, AND BE PREPARED FOR THE SCARE OF YOUR LIFE!

The night of the special event, Ken was beside himself with anticipation. He took the bus to the amusement park, but when he got there, no one was there to greet him. He walked past the open gate and through the deserted park, past unfinished rides and attractions under construction.

"Is anybody here?" he called out. But the only sound that greeted him was the *krh-krh-krh-krh* sound of a roller coaster climbing up a long first hill.

Ken ran toward the sound, then stopped in awe. There it was— the tallest, meanest, scariest-looking roller coaster he had ever seen!

The next car was pulling into the station, and Ken saw that he wasn't alone after all— another kid, a girl, was standing there, waiting for the roller coaster

car to come to a stop. Ken ran past the girl without looking at her and jumped into the very front seat, his favorite.

The thing Ken loved most about roller coasters was coming over the top of a steep hill and looking down at the long drop. It always seemed to go straight down, as if the car might bore right into the earth. Ken was thinking about this when he heard the girl's voice behind him.

"Hi, Ken," she said as the ride started.

Ken jumped. He hadn't noticed the girl getting into the car. "Uh, hi," he said, wondering where he'd heard her voice. He could swear the girl sounded just like Janey. But, no, it couldn't be . . . Janey died in the accident.

Scared to death, Ken faced forward, holding tight to the metal handrail. The roller coaster was heading up the first hill now, grinding gears as it neared the top.

"Is—is that you, Janey?" Ken asked without turning around.

"Uh-huh," Janey said. "Remember the day I died? We were sitting on that roller coaster together. You wanted it to be scarier, so you undid the seat belt. But *I* was the one who fell out, not *you*. *I* fell to the pavement, while *you* managed to hang on."

"It was an accident, Janey," Ken yelled back at the ghostly girl as the gears started grinding louder. "It wasn't my fault!"

Janey just grinned. "Well, now you're gonna get what you want. This ride is really gonna scare you. You know why? It isn't finished. There's nothing after the top of this hill."

"No!" Ken screamed.

"Don't stand up," Janey shouted over the whipping wind, "and remember to keep your arms and legs inside the car at all times."

And then Janey disappeared, leaving Ken all alone on the horrible roller coaster. The car started over the first hill and plunged into space. As Ken flew through the air, he almost had to laugh. This was the scariest ride of his life . . . and also the shortest.

I Know What You're Doing

I know who you are. I know where you live. In fact, I'm watching you this very minute.

You don't believe me?

Well, I can prove it to you. I know what you're doing right now, right this very second. In fact, I'll tell you.

You're reading the last story in this book, *More Three-Minute Thrillers*.

You think that's funny? You think it's a joke?

It's not. I'm serious. Dead serious.

I know everything about you. I knew you would get this book. Oh, I didn't know if you'd buy it yourself, or if somebody would buy it for you. I wasn't sure if you'd pick it up at a bookstore, or get it through a book club or at school—or even if you'd find it at a friend's house. I didn't know how you'd get a hold of it. I just knew that, eventually, this book would arrive in the hands of the person it was intended for . . . *you*.

Right about now you might be wondering who *I* am.

No, don't bother looking at the cover of the book. That isn't me. The author of the rest of these stories—well, let's just say I took care of him. I ripped him apart with my claws. The police thought he was killed by a wild animal—maybe you read about it? Probably not. I mean, it's not like he was R. L. Stine or Stephen King or anything. His death wasn't important enough to make the papers.

He had finished twenty-nine of the stories when I killed him. Then I sent the thirtieth story—*this* story, the one you're reading—to his bublisher.

(Sorry, I meant "publisher." It's so hard to type with these claws. It was so much easier when I used to be in human form.)

Anyway, his editor didn't know the difference, and the book was published. All I had to do was wait for you to get it.

I was watching when you picked it up for the first time. I saw you look at the cover, open the book, then start scanning it. I studied the expression on your face. I've been watching you ever since, waiting for you to reach *this* story.

You still don't believe me? You really don't think that I'm watching you right now. You think I'm making all this up.

Well, I can prove it to you . . . and I will, in less than a minute.

So maybe you're wondering why I'm doing this to you. Well, maybe I have a reason, and maybe I don't. Maybe I'll tell you, and maybe I won't . . . when I see you . . . *tonight*.

Remember? I know where you live. I know where your bedroom is. I know—

Oh, yes . . . I said I'd prove to you that I was watching you. Well, I'll prove it to you right now . . .

You just turned the page, didn't you? Yes, you did—you can't deny it! How else would you be reading this?

Anyway, don't worry. You won't know when I'll come for you, and you won't feel a thing . . . I'll just wait until you fall asleep. And then . . .